The Life of Beast

BEAST

Savage Authors LLC

Before I get started I would like to give my beautiful sister from a different mom a shout out, Yanee Brinks. Thanks for everything and I love you girl!

To my handsome boys Michael Steven Jr aka M.J. and Kairo Ilay Whiting aka Roro, you both complete me whole sons. I love you both more than you know.

To Nicholas Flores, bro thanks for believing in me. Teneka West, you're the best. Jessica Randolph, let's get it sis. If I can do it then you can do it sis.

Michael Steven Sr., this is for you babe. I see you looking down from heaven saying about damn time.

Lastly I thank God. Without God I'm nothing but a beast trying to find where she belongs in this cold world.

And to everyone else that stands with me and believes in me, thank you. Let's get this cracking. Be blessed.

CONTENTS

HERE WE GO...

Where do I begin? Oh yeah, y'all don't know me. See I'm new to this writing game. My name is Sherrell but everyone calls me ZZ. This is my new book, my life. I'm about to let y'all get to know me.

Some people may already know how I became ZZ the beast or so they think. Well sit back and let me educate you with the facts. I'm walking street testimony. Let's look back at my childhood.

CHAPTER ONE: MY GUIDANCE/CHILDHOOD

My childhood wasn't perfect. If you ever watched Cinderella then you would know my life. But I didn't have two evil sisters. Instead, I had a brother that used be a DJ. He was my guardian's only child. Maybe I shouldn't use guardian. She was more like my foster mom but she never went court.

I was a black market baby. That meant my little brother's dad gave me away to a family friend. His intent was to destroy my mom. I was her only girl. And well, it work but back to my foster mom.

She never really showed me love nor attention. She used to scream all the times so I used to stay in my room. I started reading different books about this and that. That's when writing came into my life and became my only escape. It kept me from living with the harsh reality of my life.

I used get a check every month. But of course she never spent it on me. I remember one Christmas I wanted a T-mobile Sidekick. We were at her sister's house for Christmas with other family. I watched as all my cousins got what they wanted. She told me to wait until we got back home.

My gifts were to be on the table. I was so excited. When we got home I searched for a T-Mobile Sidekick but I didn't see it. Instead she went to the store and brought me windbreakers. For those that don't know, wind-breakers are warm up pants with the matching jackets.

I was so mad. She lied to me again and in front of everyone while we were at her sister's house. To be hon-est I don't want to talk more about her nor her son in my book anymore. It's going start too much shit so next chapter.

CHAPTER TWO: RAPED AT EIGHT YEARS OLD

Some stories never leave your mind. You just put them in back of your mind and try to forget. I was raped by a man that was not my blood uncle but I looked at him as so. I unfortunately remember the day as if it were yesterday.

We went to one of my great uncles funeral. It was my guardian's uncle funeral. Being that she was surrounded by family she wasn't ready to leave. So she stayed behind. And she had asked her brother in law to take me home.

I had on this pretty little dress. But I hated dresses. He told her yeah that he would get me home safely. We were going to meet her at home and she agreed. It was a long trip back home.

He started touching me on my private parts. I didn't cry. Having this "gift" you see things before it happens. We finally got to my house. I had a key at an early age so he took my key and unlocked the door. Next thing I knew he had followed me to my room and made me take off my clothes. That's when he first raped me.

After he was done he did the typical rapist thing and he told me take a bath. I did. After that he dried me off. By that time my guardian had come home. My clothes were already in the bathroom. And he was talking to her.

I came out of my room to find him and her talking. He looked at me and smiled. I wanted to kill him. I never told my guidance what happened because she wouldn't have cared nor believed me anyway. And she still don't know where that dress is to this day.

I burned it in front of that house. That why I don't like surprises nor do I smile anymore. I was a somewhat happy girl until that happened.

CHAPTER THREE: MY GIFT

I never understood my gift until I got older. I see, feel, and smell things before it happens. I also see dead people and new people before I meet them. I hated my gift growing up. Family members and friends thought I was weird and a demon.

I used watch my guardian sleep. She used to be afraid of me. I just wanted to know how she slept at night knowing that she treated me so badly. Example: I knew I was going to get raped and by who. I knew that my little brother's dad was full of shit. I pretty much knew everything.

I just didn't say shit. I learn my words are powerful. So I don't waste them on nonsense people. That's why I don't talk that much unless I have something important to say. Another reason is that not everyone understands me for me. This gift causes me to stay single too. Maybe I'll meet that person one day when I'm not looking for him or her.

CHAPTER FOUR: SO MANY NAMES BUT ONLY ONE ME

I have so many names people called me. Sherrell, Rell, Sha Sha, Sha, Rude Boi, X-Ecstasy, X, R.B.(short for Rude Boi), Z, ZZ, S. Nichole, Nichole, and now Beast. To be honest I used to hate my name. But now it's okay.

I don't like when people call me by my government name. Some can't even pronounce it. I'm named after my mom. Her name is Cheryl. So that's her way of naming me after her.

If I let you call me by my government name that means you're special to me. That's a privilege that many don't get. I would rather be called Z, ZZ, or Beast because my names hold volumes.

CHAPTER FIVE: I HATED SCHOOL

School and I didn't get along because English isn't my first language. My little brother's dad taught me another language growing up. It was French. My real mom didn't like that at all. I used to get bullied which turned me into one.

Elementary wasn't bad. My guardian, her niece, her niece's two boys, and I moved to Port Arthur, Texas. They went to Lincoln and I went to Robert E. Lee. My grades were okay for the most part. But after a while they moved back to Louisiana and later we moved to Beaumont.

Our house in Port Arthur used to be haunted. Or at least I used to see things and people. It was a three bedroom and two bathroom house. My guardian had her own room, her niece had her own room, then my cousin and I shared a room. I didn't like that either. If only these walls could talk...hmm. Smh

CHAPTER SIX: MOVING TO BEAUMONT

Beaumont used to be on the map. Beaumont was the place to move to. We used to have block parties. The neighbors used to keep an eye on you and your kids. And there wasn't that much crime.

We used to stay on Hartel Street in South Park. It was a white house that has two bedrooms and one bathroom. It was small with a nice yard. I had a basketball hoop out back. Man, I thought I was Sheryl Swoopes and Tina Thompson.

Those are my two favorite female players. Plus, I love watching the Bulls. I'm a huge Chicago Bulls fan. Michael Jordan was and still is my favorite player too. That's one of my reasons why my favorite colors are red and black.

I played basketball in middle school. I used to be so cold at it too. I was a point guard dreaming that I'll make it one day. That dream died when they didn't let me play in my eighth grade year because my age.

So I quit playing. They wanted me to play for high school, but it was too late. Those days were behind me. Although, I find myself trying to find that drive to play again. But it's not there anymore. Maybe one day. Who knows!

CHAPTER SEVEN: MY MOM AND UNCLE KNEW I WAS GOING BE GAY

When my mom did raise me, my uncle and her knew I was going to be gay. I used to buy candies for girls when I was in elementary. Being raped didn't make me gay. It was my choice to be gay. And no, I'm not bisexual either.

I like having sex with guys, but I love females. If I could I would married a bisexual guy and gay female. But you can't. I call it open when you want both men and women at the same time. In society they called it bisexual.

I don't see myself going out with a man. But a female, yes. My uncle used to always say I was his boy. Rest in Peace Uncle Freddy. He was my favorite uncle. He died two years ago.

I don't like too many females that I see. I have a lot of boundaries and standards. I love females with minds and not just a body. And I like guys with big butts. Not a fat guy, but a guy that work out like me. Until I find the one who understand me for me. I'm staying single.

CHAPTER EIGHT: TEENAGE YEARS

I went to Ozen High School in Beaumont when I was a teenager. Everyone knew me. I was popular you could say. I used to play softball. I was a shortstop and my number was 23.

I played three years from ninth grade to eleven grade. Plus, I did chess club. My first baby daddy taught me how to play. I don't know how to play checkers nor dominoes, but chess yes. It's my favorite board game.

I didn't go to prom nor other dances in high school. But I did join ROTC. Only in 9th grade though. It wasn't for me. Plus I was too busy being drug dealer in school.

I used to sell to the teachers, students, principals, and cafeteria workers. I never got into trouble. At least not for selling drugs but I did for skipping school. I often went to all three lunches. Those were my happy times of Beast in the making.

CHAPTER NINE: MY OLDEST CHILD'S DAD

He was a friend of the family. He's the one that moved my guardian and me to Beaumont. He was my protector from her and the world. My guardian used to be so mean. She never said, "I love you." That hurt a lot.

She used to stay going back and forward to Louisiana. I stayed with him a lot of the time. Although he had sickle cell. Some female put their men in front their kids or child. She was one of those women.

She used to cook for him while I had cereal and noodles. That's why I don't like cereals and noodles now. I hardly have these things in my house now until my oldest comes home to visit. But this was a sweet man. He cooked, cleaned, and took care of the outside.

To be honest I don't wanted get in more detail about

him. It's too much for me right now. Let him Rest In
Peace.

him. It's too much for me right now. Let him Rest In
Peace.

CHAPTER TEN: HAVING MY FIRST CHILD AT TWENTY-TWO

I used to be a cheater. I cheated on my oldest child's dad when I went to visit my real mom. She wasn't coming around and I didn't see or hear from her. We left Franklin and my oldest child's dad and I move to Baytown after I graduated high school. We stayed at Bay Harbor Apartments in Baytown on Alexander Street.

We had an upstairs apartment. It was two bedrooms and one bathroom. It was huge. So one day my son's dad said, "I think you should go visit your mom." I agreed with him. I went and stayed a week.

I saw this white man that worked at a restaurant in Patterson, Louisiana. If you know me then you know that if I see something or someone I like I'm gone get it. He had braids with a neck tattoo that said only God can judge me. I told my real mom, her boyfriend at the time, and my little brother that he's going to be my babydaddy.

I gave him my mom's phone number because I didn't have a phone at time. He called me when he got off work. He walked to my mom's apartment. My little brother was jealous because he couldn't have females over. I was a brat. Still is in some sense.

We did it. It was okay. Once I found out I was pregnant I thought it was him. But it wasn't him that was my oldest child's father. It was my old dude back in Texas. That's how oatmeal cookie came about.(laugh out loud)

But I'm not a cheater no more. I was young and stupid. Now I'm single and having time of my life. It's just God, my kids, and me.

CHAPTER ELEVEN: POF (PLENTY OF FUCKS)

I never liked dating apps. But one of my homegirls told me about this one app. It was called POF. So I tried it. I met a lot of females on there. Some were gold diggers and others were full of shit.

I met this beautiful femme. She was staying in Crosby, Texas. I think I spelled Crosby wrong. But anyway, she was so beautiful. Everyone told me to stay away from her. They said that she was no good.

But I didn't listen. We used to fight a lot. She was so toxic. She stole my car and went to Houston while I stayed in Dallas. To make matters worse I was homeless for seven months.

I lost everything including my pride and my son. My son ended up staying with his dad. That's another story for another day. But her and I didn't even last a month. I broke up with her and end up moving back to Beaumont with my guardian.

Moving on I met this chick and she was already pregnant. Well I'm going to talk about her in the next chapter. Stay tuned. But POF is trash. If you read my first book "This Fucking Love Shit" then you already know why. But I still am on there as I_am_beast. Hit me up sometime. (Laughing to myself.)

CHAPTER TWELVE: WHAT WAS I THINKING

I met this girl on POF and she was already pregnant. I didn't have my second born yet. She had just moved back with her mom from Dallas. Or so she claimed. But I think that was a lie.

I didn't know she was bisexual until three years into our friendship. Her mom stayed next to my guardian's house in South Park. We talked awhile on PoF. We did that until she was ready to meet me. I'll never forget that day.

It was raining that day. I had just gotten off work. I used to work at a hospital as a deli maker. Man I miss that job. But anyway she was about five months pregnant, I think.

My play brother Reggie and I went to the mall and we

ate at Taco Bell. She finally sent me a message saying to come get her. I dropped him off and went to get her. She wanted some Taco Bell too. I guess since that's the place my play brother and I ate from.

So I wasn't hungry but I paid for it. We ended up going to the mall too. We sat by the coffee place. She ate her food. After that we walked around a bit. I made her a bear from Build A Bear and bought us rings.

We made that bear together. I put a special heart in him. It quoted I will never leave you. Well years later and she's still on that stupid shit and we stayed on this crazy roll coaster. I decided to get off this ride with her. Now she's pregnant with her second child. She's having another girl. Congratulations to her. Life goes on without her.

CHAPTER THIRTEEN: MY SECOND BORN DEADBEAT DAD

We used to work together at City of Beaumont. He was the lead and I was the laborer. We worked at Sport Complex. He's older than me. He's in his forties. I'm in my early thirties.

He's brown skinned and has one bad leg. His right leg is bad because he used to ride horses back in the day. This was before Kairo was born. He has an older daughter and teenage son. Yep, they are by different baby mommas.

I liked him so I started dressing like a female. Trying walk straight, but I'm not a straight person. It feels funny being a girly girl. So, I told him I just wanted to fuck. That was cool with him.

He smoked a lot of weed and drinks a lot too. He was staying with his dad until they built his dad a new home. I helped him find an apartment for his daughter and him. I realized that I didn't like him nor love him. He was a hoe.

Out of all the women he was playing with I'm the only one that got pregnant. When I had the baby he saw Kairo one time. Kairo was one week old. He brought two packages of diapers. I decided to put him on child support. But the system is sorry.

I still don't get child support for Kairo. Kairo is about to be two in August. His dad is a sorry ass nigga. But Kairo is my blessing. So I thank his dad for him.

CHAPTER FOURTEEN:

There's no chapter fourteen. I hope y'all enjoyed my book. Maybe I'll write a part 2. Who knows? Until the pen hit the paper, be blessed y'all.

ABOUT THE AUTHOR

Beast

I am Beast. I live in Beaumont, Texas and I'm single with two children that I love more than life itself. My love of reading set on early in life. Although I love reading that's not what got me into writing. My life has hosted many events and left me with many thoughts. I would often write my own things but I never published them. I finally decided to share my struggles and views on life so This Fucking Love Shit is my first book, my baby. I welcome all to follow me as I continue to deliver you the raw uncut views and opinions of my life experiences.

BOOKS BY THIS AUTHOR

The Life Of Beast

This Fucking Love Shit is a look into my life and is my raw opinion on love. In this book you will get insight into why I feel the way I do about love. I share my personal stories with you. I keep it real with you throughout the entire book.

Dive into this Fucking love shit and see how "Beast" was created.

FOLLOW ME

Be sure to follow me for my newest releases and up-dates!

www.Facebook.com/AuthorBeast

Amazon.com/author/zzbeast